# So She Did

Dr. Aleen Kojayan

Jade is not like most other first graders in town. Unlike her classmates, Jade does not like to dance or play basketball. She does not enjoy drawing or singing, but she does love cars.

There are two things Jade loves more than anything: her family and cars.

Cars! Cars! Cars!
In Jade's room there are toy cars on the floor, on the wall, and even on the shelves.

Jade spends hours playing with her toy cars.
Big, small, fast, slow, and in every possible color.
Her bright blue eyes light up when she sees all
the toy cars in her room.

Jade's love for cars began at
her parents' shop, GC Automotives.
GC is a small family mechanic shop.
All customers are treated like family.

Every summer since she was born,
Jade has spent most of her days
at her parents' mechanic shop.

During the summer, Jade's parents pick up a coffee for them and a donut for her as they drive into the shop. Jade's favorite is a rainbow sprinkle donut with a bottle of chocolate milk to wash it down.
On the way to the shop, she loves to roll down the windows, feeling the wind through her soft brown hair.
CENTRAL BANK
HOTEL

Jade's mother and father work together.
While one works at the front desk,
the other keeps an eye on Jade,
keeping her away from the tools and
dirt of the cars.
OIL

Her parents do their best to keep Jade in the front office, but somehow she always makes her way to the garage.
OIL

Jade has always been interested
in working on cars.
She used to watch her parents
at the shop, then come home
and do the same on her toy cars.
For her it was like putting
together the pieces of a puzzle.

Occasionally her parents would let her use the tools at their shop. This made Jade so happy!
OIL

It is the first day of school and Jade is excited to show her classmates all that she has learned over the summer.

Ring! Ring!
Jade's teacher Mrs. Sparks welcomes the class to first grade.
"We are going to go around and introduce ourselves," says Mrs. Sparks. "Please tell us your name and what you want to be when you grow up."

The teacher calls on Jade to begin.
Jade nervously stands up in front of all
her new classmates.
"Hi, my name is Jade, and I want to be a
mechanic when I grow up."

All Jade's classmates start laughing.
"That's not a job for girls!" they say.

Mrs. Sparks quickly asks the students to quiet down.
Embarrassed, Jade returns to her seat
with her face as red as a tomato.

Jade spends the entire day wondering
why her classmate laughed at her.
She loves watching not only her father,
but also her mother work on cars,
so why shouldn't she?

Frustrated, Jade throws all her toy cars into
the trash. She thinks that in order
to fit in, she must give up her passion for cars.

The next morning, Jade's father notices all her cars in the trash.
He says to Jade, "What are all of your cars doing in the trash?"
She responds, "I threw them away because girls are not supposed to play with cars."

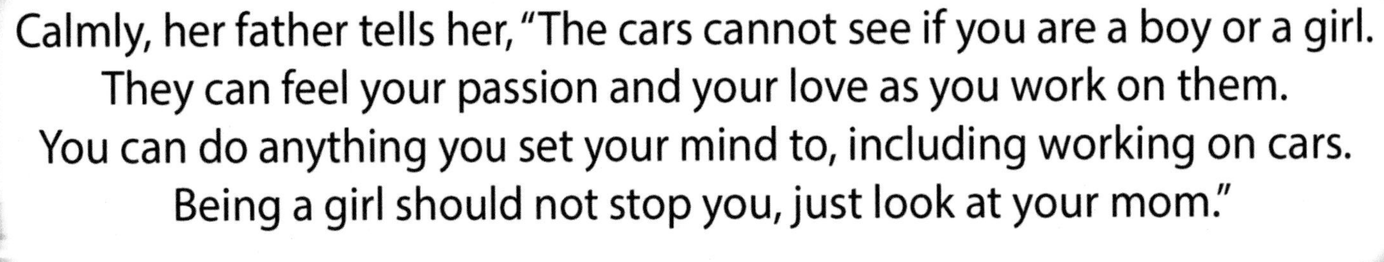

Calmly, her father tells her, "The cars cannot see if you are a boy or a girl. They can feel your passion and your love as you work on them. You can do anything you set your mind to, including working on cars. Being a girl should not stop you, just look at your mom."

So she does.
Jade goes to the trash,
takes out all of her cars,
puts them in her backpack,
and goes to school.

Jade walks into school feeling more confident than ever. She holds her head up high and walks through the front doors of her classroom.

Jade approaches Mrs. Sparks and says, "I would like to reintroduce myself to the class."
With a huge smile on her face her teacher says, "That is a great idea."

Mrs. Sparks announces to the class,
"Jade has something important
to share with you all."

Jade stands up from her desk and confidently says,
"Hi, my name is Jade and when I grow up,
I want to be a mechanic."

And so she did.
Jade is looking forward to going on this journey with you to learn all there is to know about cars.